For my fellow LMNO pea-brains, AW (editor!) and SC (designer!).
And special thanks to LC (friend!), a true pea-liever.

BEACH LANE BOOKS • An imprint of Simon & Schuster Children's Publishing Division •
1230 Avenue of the Americas, New York, New York 10020 • Copyright © 2017 by Keith
Baker • All rights reserved, including the right of reproduction in whole or in part in any form.
• BEACH LANE BOOKS is a trademark of Simon & Schuster, Inc. • For information about special
discounts for bulk purchases, please contact Simon & Schuster Special Sales at 1-866-506-1949 or
business@simonandschuster.com. • The Simon & Schuster Speakers Bureau can bring authors to
your live event. For more information or to book an event, contact the Simon & Schuster Speakers
Bureau at 1-866-248-3049 or visit our website at www.simonspeakers.com. • Book design by
Sonia Chaghatzbanian • The text for this book was set in Frankfurter Medium. • Manufactured in
China • 0517 SCP • First Edition • CIP data is available from the Library of Congress. • ISBN 978-
1-4814-5856-6 (hardcover) • ISBN 978-1-4814-5857-3 (eBook) • 10 9 8 7 6 5 4 3 2 1

LMNO pea-quel

keith baker

Beach Lane Books New York London Toronto Sydney New Delhi

We are peas—alphabet peas!
We're busy *again* in the **ab**cs.

We're architects,

authors,

and actors, you and I.

We're botanists

and bakers—how 'bout a berry pie?

We're cleaners

and cowpokes—who here wants a ride?

We're doormen at your service and dentists—*open wide!*

We're engineers
at the wheel
of a speedy train.

We're firefighters
on the job

and field hands—is that rain?

We're golfers on the greens—

We're groomers

and garbage collectors—
our work is never done.

We're hairdressers,

hippies,

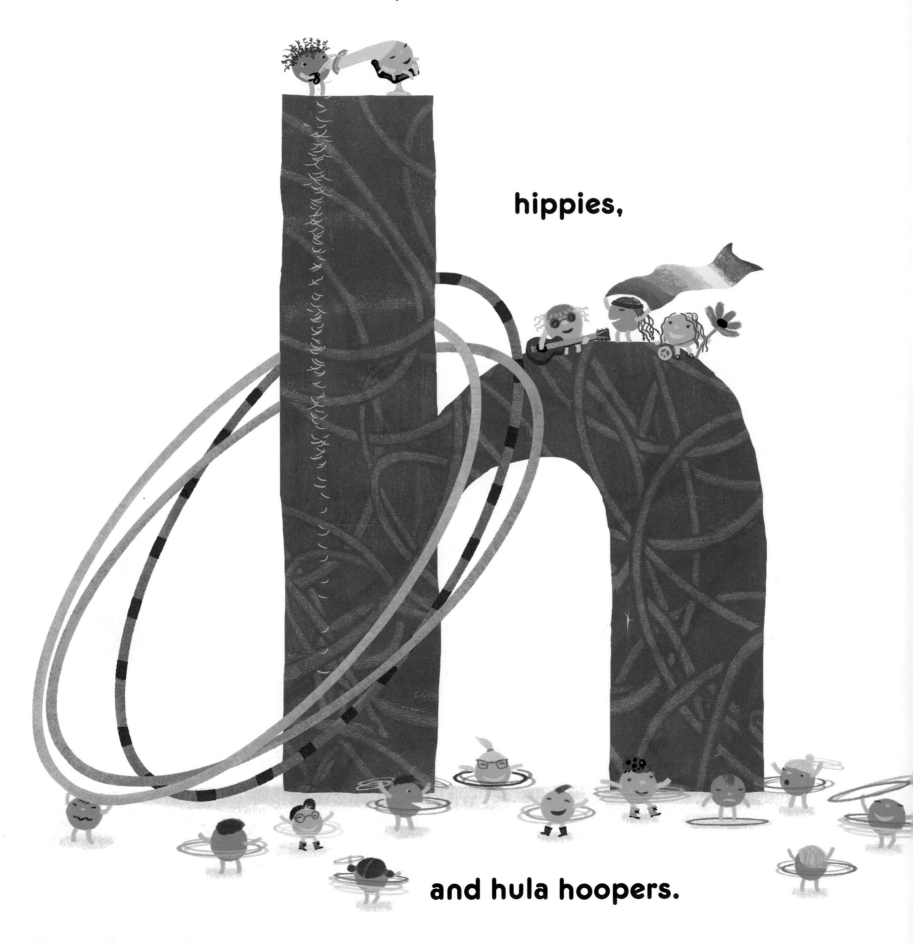

and hula hoopers.

**We're ichthyologists—
we study fish!—**

**and we're
ice-cream scoopers.**

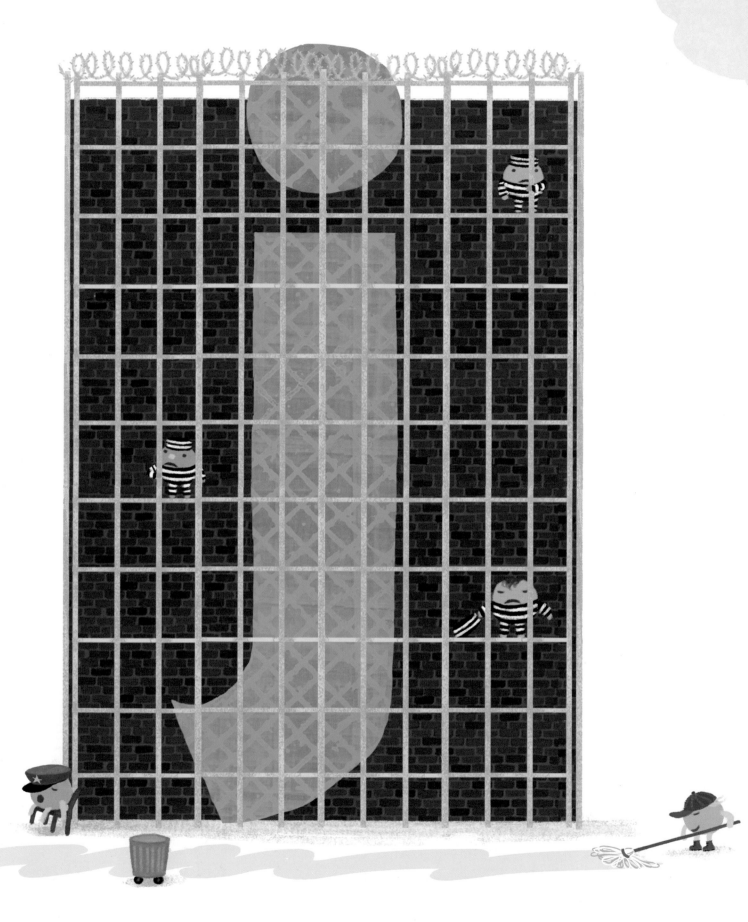

We're jailbirds and janitors,

kite gliders
on the breeze.

We're loggers sawing logs

and locksmiths cutting keys.

We're mothers making lists,

newborns,

and optometrists.

We're pirates on the open seas—

Aaaaaarrrrrgggghhh—
so mad and mean!

And one—and only one of us!—

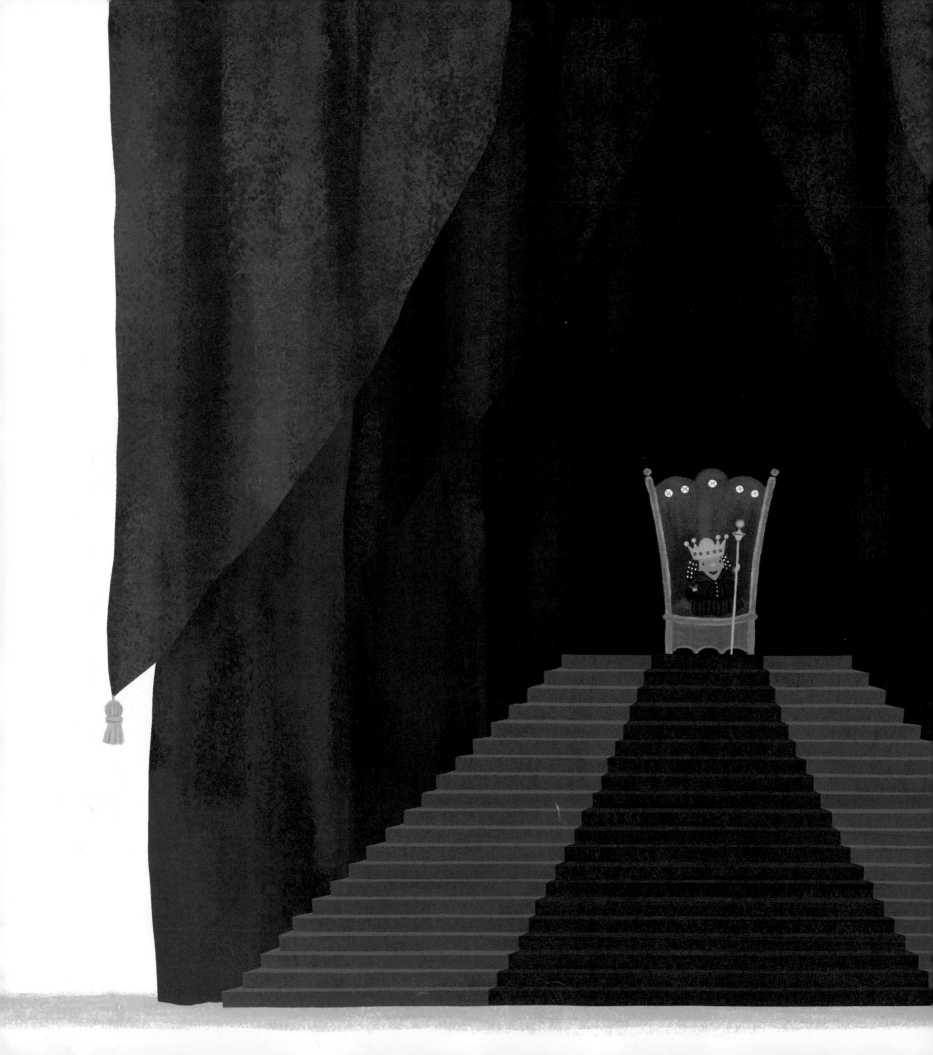

is the royal queen.

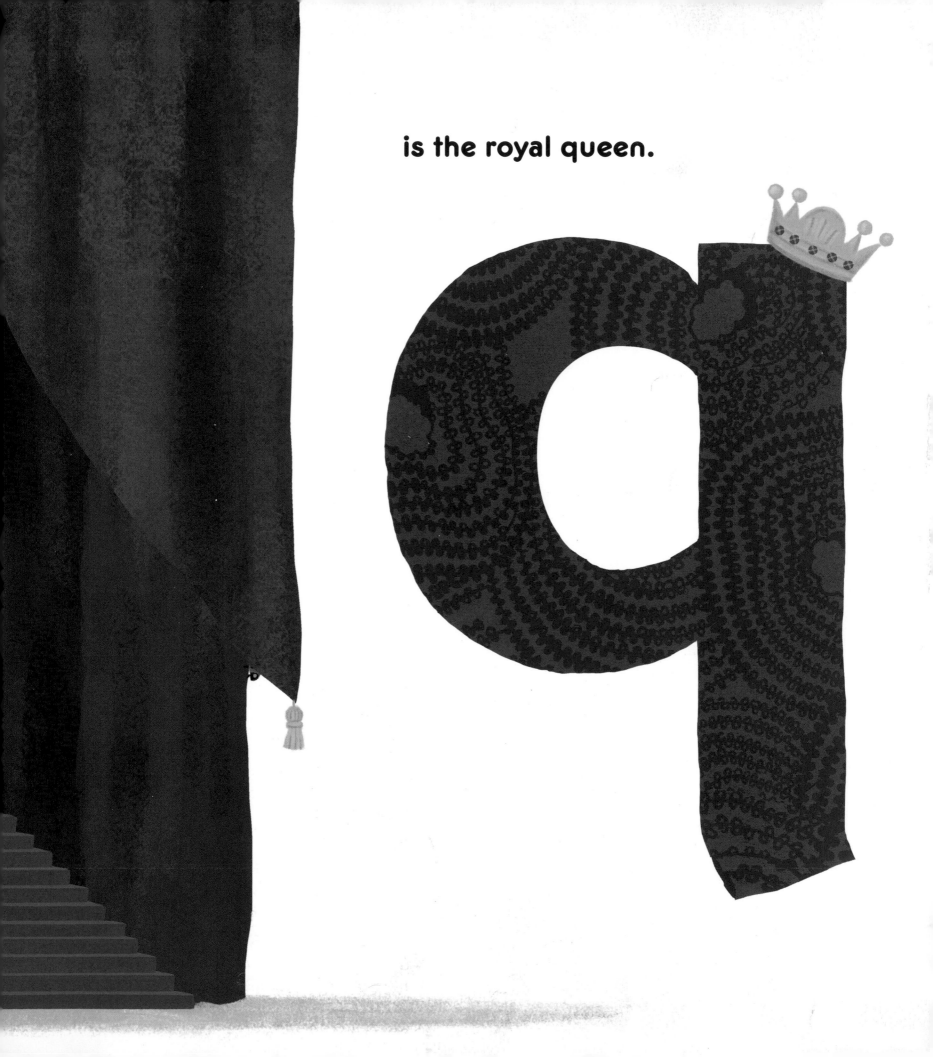

We're roofers,

rappers,

soldiers in a row,

SCHOOL

students, and tailors—*sew, sew, sew!*

We're umpires,

uncles (yes, we're aunties too),

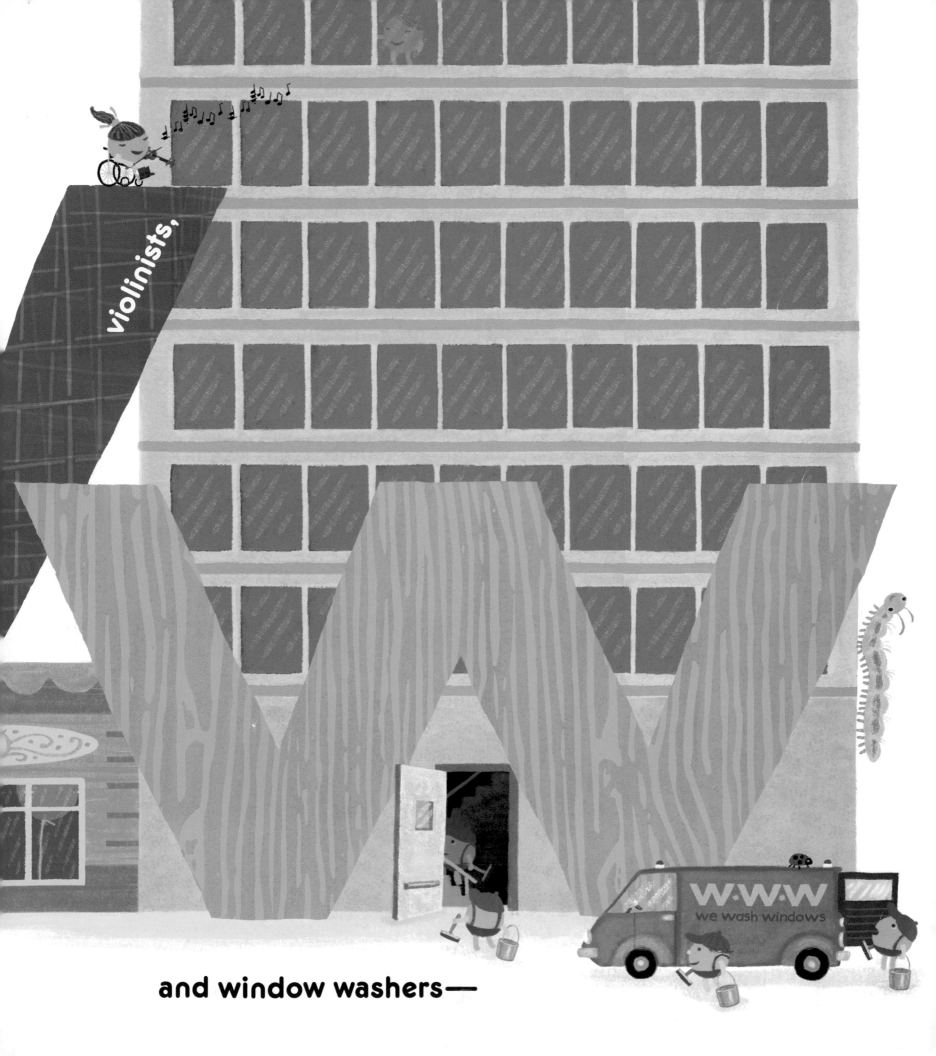

violinists,

and window washers—

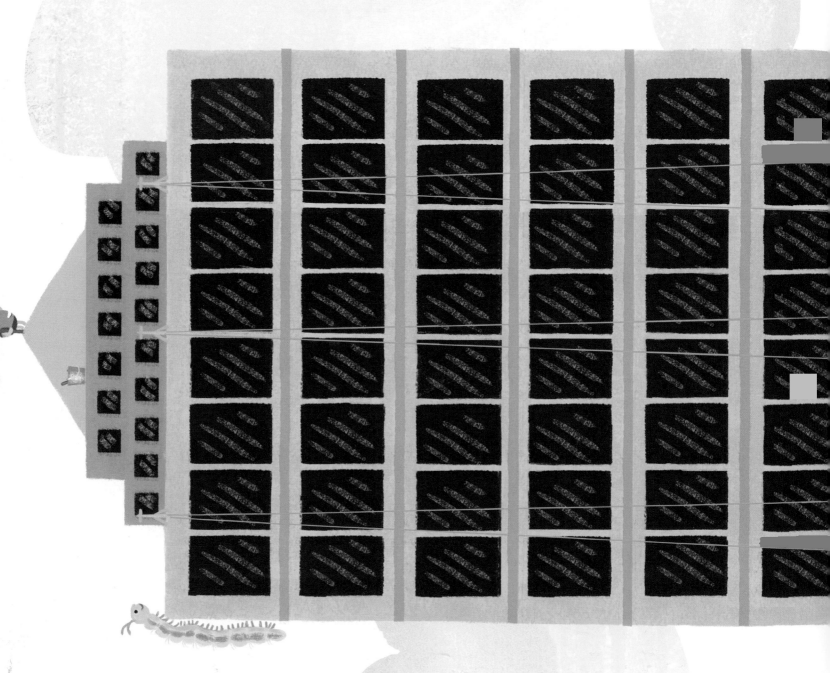

Wow, what a view!

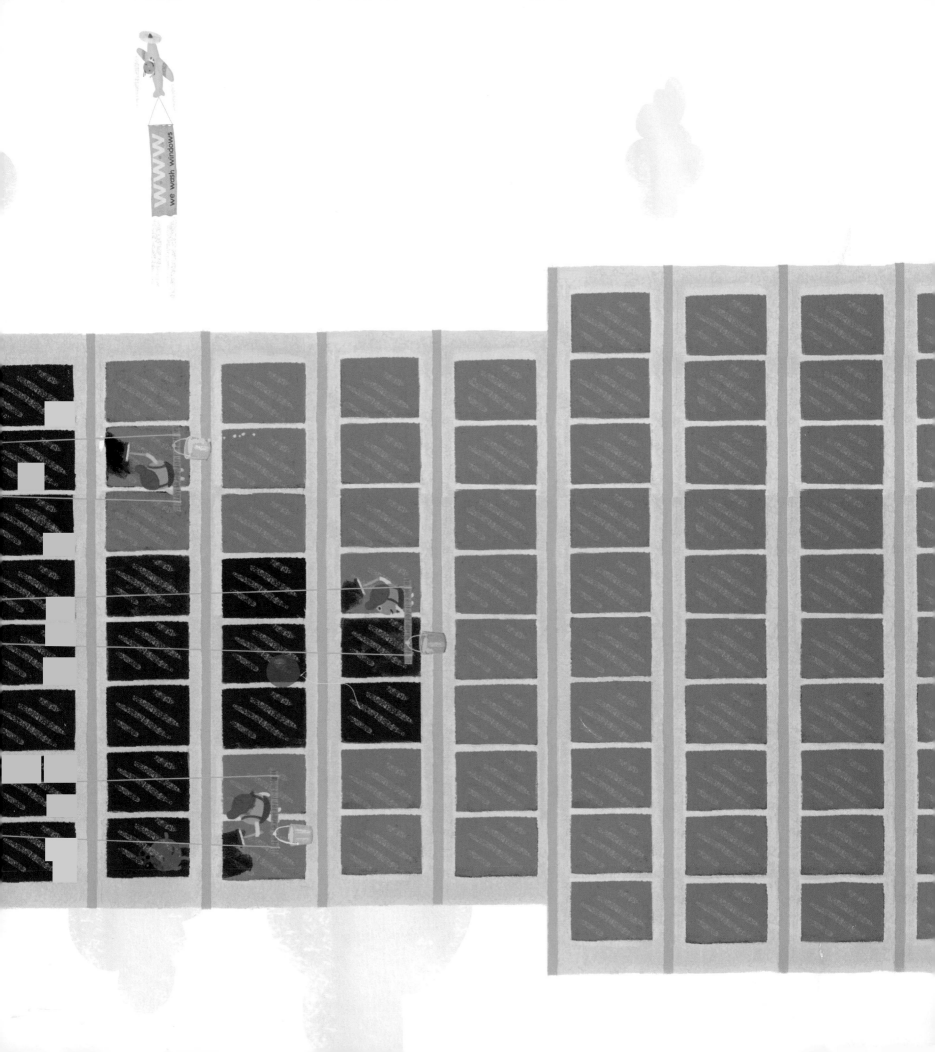

We're X-Peas to the rescue—

We're yakkers on our phones—
yak, yak, yak, yak, yak!

We're zippers
on a zip line,
zipping over—

and back!

And we're dreamers, too, throughout the abcs.
What will we be now?

So many